Back to the Manger

A TREASURE HUNT FOR THE NATIVITY

Margaret Ann Philbrick   *Illustrated by* Sarah Ellen McGreevy

Singing River Publications, Inc.
Ely, Minnesota

Published by
Singing River Publications, Inc.
PO Box 72, Ely, Minnesota 55731
www.singingriverpublications.com

Book design by Dorie McClelland
Printed in Canada

ISBN: 978-0-9789870-8-4
LCCN pending

We are so grateful to these friends
who helped make this book dream
a reality: Suzanne P. Massion,
Tim Morgan, Christine Moroni,
LaVonne Neff, Charlie Philbrick,
Katherine Ruch and our Lord and
Savior, Jesus Christ who is the
author of every story.

For the Raftery family,
The Little Traveler,
The Geneva History Center and
Inga the pie baker,
all of whom have brought us so much joy.

Every Advent season, Inga, her brother Karl, their mother and grandmother walked up the big hill to The Little Traveler gift shop to celebrate their favorite holiday tradition.

The Little Traveler is a stately, white, Victorian house in Geneva, Illinois. It is filled with treasures from all over the world. Of all the specialty shops on Third Street, The Little Traveler is the most beautiful. Each of its many rooms features gifts from different countries and cultures. Inga and her brother often played silent hide and seek among the fine linens of England and antiques from France, pretending the store was their own home.

That day there would be no hide and seek. Mother and Grandma would be watching. The children would be treated to a lunch in the fancy room, not the little café with sandwiches. This was the room which was decorated for Christmas with silver place settings and garlands of mistletoe. Momma and Grandma were looking for their best manners. If they were good, after lunch they would be allowed to stand before the "flying manger."

Inga called it the flying manger because of the multitude of royal angels that floated over the nativity scene. Along Third Street, many manger scenes were displayed but none had a heavenly host of angels that flew over Mary, Joseph and the Baby Jesus. This crèche had traveled across the ocean, all the way from Naples, Italy.

The kings are dressed in brightly colored silk. The shepherds are kind and loving, not afraid. Mary and Joseph, dressed as a king and queen in fine robes, look peacefully down on their child in the manger.

Smiling townspeople bringing their gifts surround the Holy Family. The baker brings a basket of bread; the fishmonger a creel of fish. All stand upon a bed of fine gold satin and fresh green moss. They are gathered within a rich walnut daybed covered in cedar boughs. Throughout their childhood, Inga and Karl were blessed to stand before this nativity in wonder.

Eventually, Karl and Inga grew up and moved away. Still, each Advent and Christmastime, many children continued to be delighted by the manger scene.

Years later, when Inga had a family of her own, she remembered the manger and Advent tradition. She longed for her children to experience this special time of wonder and love from her childhood.

So one Advent, she brought them to The Little Traveler. After enjoying the delicious lunch, and using please and thank you, it was time to visit the nativity scene. This nativity visit made the whole trip special. However, after searching through many rooms, they sadly realized that the manger scene was gone!

"Do you know where they have taken it?" Inga asked the clerk.

"It was donated to someone. I'm sorry but I don't know to whom," the clerk replied.

Inga wondered how something so beautiful and so full of Christmas could be given away without a thought. They set off for home in a dreary winter drizzle. Quietly, Inga promised herself that she would find the flying manger.

Inga considered all the places in town which might provide a new home for the manger. What kind of place would allow many people to come and see it? She remembered that the library often set up a nativity scene at Christmas. They would certainly be honored to have one as old and colorful as the flying manger!

The librarian told her that the library nativity scene had just been set up downstairs. Inga crossed her fingers inside her coat pocket as she raced down the steps. At the familiar children's corner, she spotted delicately carved olive wood figures, all standing inside a brown wooden stable covered with a straw roof. There was not a single angel flying overhead.

Next she thought of the big red courthouse on Third Street. Every season, the courthouse set up a life sized nativity scene on the front lawn. But like so many old traditions, it had been taken away in recent years and replaced by the evergreen-draped trailer of Santa Claus. Perhaps if the courthouse knew what had happened to their own manger, they might know about the flying manger as well.

Marching past the canons into the courthouse, Inga inquired of the courtroom clerk, "I am looking for a very special nativity scene that is missing. Do you know where they might have taken it?"

Kindly, the clerk replied that their nativity set had been donated to the Lutheran church in town. Perhaps the flying manger had found a home in another church as well.

Inga thought about how old the flying manger was. It was brought to The Little Traveler in the 1920s but created in Italy hundreds of years earlier. As she realized that this creation of Jesus, Mary and Joseph and all of their friends was several hundred years old, she decided to look in one of the oldest churches in town, St. Mark's Episcopal Church. Approaching the red arched doorway, Inga found the sexton standing outside, sweeping snow off the front steps.

"Excuse me sir. I am looking for a very special nativity scene that is lost. I am hoping that you might know something about it."

The sexton introduced himself as Mr. James Johanson and yes, he did know something about it. He led Inga into the quiet church. The only sound was that of the winter wind chiming against the stained glass windows.

As they moved through the pews toward the front, Inga spotted a small children's altar covered in cedar greens. There upon the altar was a royal manger scene. It was carved out of white alabaster and placed upon red velvet. In the soft light, the Holy Family smiled at Inga. The figures announced the Christmas story . . . but not a single angel flew overhead.

Mr. Johanson could see that Inga did not recognize the scene. "I am sorry this is not the one you are seeking."

As Inga left the church she said a quiet prayer. "Please God, help me to find your Holy Family and your host of heavenly angels. I want my own children to see them and know You."

Many happy Christmases came and went. Inga's children grew tall. Yet, she did not give up her search.

One rainy fall afternoon as Inga drove downhill toward Main Street Bridge, she saw The Little Traveler's delivery truck parked outside a riverside storage building. Two delivery men were hoisting a dark, heavy wooden piece of intricately carved furniture into the truck. In a single breath and blink, Inga recognized it! It was the French daybed which had housed the flying manger so many years before! "Perhaps if the bed is here, there might be more," she joyfully whispered to herself. Quickly she hurried to reach the delivery man and followed him inside.

A harsh voice halted her. "There's been a flood down in the basement. River water everywhere. There's nothing for the public here unless you want to help clean up."

Inga's children were in school. She could certainly spare an hour to help out. So she followed the delivery man with his squeaking rubber boots down the stairwell and into the dark basement.

As she stood knee-deep in water, the foul smell of river water filled her nose. She was staring at a soaking wet treasure trove of old furniture and chandeliers. Little pink bags were floating on top of the standing water. All of these things were cast-offs which The Little Traveler proprietors had decided to store away and sell another day.

It was hard to see in the darkness, so Inga waded over to a window well. In the scattered light, she saw a tiny person floating face up, delicate arms outstretched. A damp chill ran through her as she reached for this tiny creature. Then, she drew a doll out of the water.

Wiping mud from its face, Inga looked at the doll. The doll looked up at Inga. Its golden hair was matted with mire. Soft, brightly colored robes were spotted and stained by dirty water. As Inga turned it over, she saw that the doll had small, fragile wings caked with years of dirt. Once they shimmered. Now they were soaked with river water and dull with mud. Angel wings had turned to earth.

Standing there in the water, Inga felt her tears make a warm path down her cheeks. *She had found an angel from the flying manger.*

Quickly now, sloshing her hands through the watery mud, Inga felt many hard things that she could not see. She pulled one up and discovered a large pink and white striped box, sealed shut. She opened it. There, under the lid were Baby Jesus, Mary, and Joseph. She recognized the Holy Family that she had seen in The Little Traveler many years before. She had found the flying manger.

As she stood in the water hugging the pink and white striped box, she called out to the delivery man, "Could you help me? I've found something precious that has been lost for a very long time."

Now each Christmas, Inga, her husband Charles and their three children visit the flying manger. In all of its ancient and regal finery, it lives in the Geneva History Center on Third Street. The friendly shepherds and townspeople all smile. The kings exalt in finding the Christ. The Holy Family peacefully rests upon a bed of fine gold satin and fresh green moss. Above them fly a multitude of heavenly angels. If you listen very carefully, you can hear them sing,

"Glory to God in the highest and on earth peace, goodwill toward men."

Note to the Reader:

The Neapolitan crèche described in this story was created in Naples, Italy, during the 1700s. In addition to the intricate traditional nativity characters depicted, the artistic creators embellished the scene with townspeople bringing gifts, creating a celebration for the Holy Family. This nativity set was developed by a number of master craftsmen, each of whom specialized in a particular artistic piece of the display. Lorenzo Mosca created the shepherds. Trilocco and Saverio Vassallo fashioned the animals out of terra cotta. Vinaccia was renowned for his small stringed instruments made of wood or mother of pearl. All of Naples was involved in the exhibit of nativity scenes because the aristocracy competed to have the most elaborate and imaginative scene.

Three weeks before Christmas, churches and palaces in Christendom were open to the common folk so that all could view this art form and worship the Christ Child. Since the common folk were not formally educated and most of them did not read, visual art was the instructional forum for Christianity. In 1734, King Charles III of Naples created a depth perspective in the arrangement of his display while the Queen spent the year sewing costumes for the palace figures.

During the 1920s, Kate Raftery, founder of The Little Traveler, purchased one of these nativity scenes. The figures and the French walnut daybed were shipped from overseas and arrived by train at the Geneva, Illinois depot. For many decades, the crèche was displayed on a bed of fine gold satin and fresh green moss at The Little Traveler.

Eventually, the nativity set fell into a state of disrepair and was stored in the basement of a shop on River Lane, right next to the Fox River. For many years its location was not known. It was "lost" until the late 1960s when Mr. Merritt King, a former Geneva, Illinois alderman and historian found the bed and figures. The building which stored the crèche was scheduled for demolition. Mr. King had been sent into its basement to see if the heating oil tanks were empty and electricity was turned off.

Wearing rubber boots, he descended the stairway into the basement where he encountered a foot of water. Floating on the surface of the water were many pink bags from The Little Traveler. Mr. King saw the French daybed standing in the water wrapped in newspaper. He removed a pink and white striped box from the water and found the nativity figures.

"It was a miracle that they were still intact and had not been chewed to bits by rats and mice," he said.

Mr. King brought them home and dried them out in his oven. Then he contacted The Little Traveler.

In 1971, the Simon family purchased The Little Traveler and once again the crèche was displayed there. In 1989, The Little Traveler donated the figures to The Geneva History Center with the goal of complete restoration. The partially restored crèche is now displayed from Thanksgiving to New Year's Day in their museum at 113 South Third Street, Geneva, Illinois. The restoration is ongoing. Donors are still being sought to complete the project. If you are interested in contributing to this crèche restoration, please contact The Geneva History Center at 639-232-4961 or at www.genevahistorycenter.org.

Source: *The Nativity, The Christmas Crèche at The Metropolitan Museum of Art*, Doubleday and Company, New York, 1965